D0004263

MOUSE AND MOLE

FINE FEATHERED FRIENDS

WONG HERBERT YEE

HOUGHTON MIFFLIN BOOKS FOR CHILDREN
HOUGHTON MIFFLIN HARCOURT
BOSTON NEW YORK 2009

For bird lovers, young and old

www.hmhbooks.com

The text of this book is set in Adobe Caslon.
The illustrations are litho pencil and gouache.

Library of Congress Cataloging-in-Publication Data
Yee, Wong Herbert.
Mouse and Mole, fine feathered friends / by Wong Herbert Yee.
p. cm.
"Houghton Mifflin Books for Children."
Summary: When spring arrives, Mole and Mouse find a unique way to bird watch.
ISBN 978-0-547-15222-6
[1. Bird watching—Fiction. 2. Birds—Fiction.
3. Mice—Fiction. 4. Moles (Animals)—Fiction.
5. Spring—Fiction.] I. Title.
PZ7.Y3655Mo 2009
[E]—dc22
2008040465

Printed in Singapore
TWP 10 9 8 7 6 5 4 3 2 1

CONTENTS

BIRD BOOKS

Spring was Mole's favorite time of year.

Spring was when the birds came back.

Mole was simply *mad* about birds!

He opened the door a crack —

whoosh! A gust of wind

blew his hat off.

"Yikes!" cried Mole.

He ran to pick it up.

Meanwhile . . .
Mouse peeked
behind boxes.

Mouse peered
inside bags.

"Aha!" Mouse cried. She yanked her
backpack off the top shelf.

Mouse put a sketchpad in the big pocket.

She stuffed crayons
in the little pocket.

TAP-TAP-TAP.

Mouse heard
someone knocking.

She opened the door a crack — *whoosh!*

A gust of wind blew it wide open.

"My, what a blustery day!" she squeaked.

Mouse tied a bonnet
on her head.

"Morning, Mouse!" said Mole.

"All set to work on our bird books?"

"I packed my sketchpad and crayons,"
said Mouse. "I have binoculars, too!
Where should we look first?"

Mole rubbed his snout.

"Birds hide in bushes," he said.

"Let's try the huckleberry."

Mouse looked to her left.

Mole looked to his right.

There were no birds in sight.

"Come out, come out, wherever

you are!" Mouse sang.

"Quiet!" shushed Mole.

"Birds nest in trees,"

he whispered.

"Let's check

under the pines."

Mole peered up at the branches.

"A pine siskin!" Mole pointed.

Mouse looked through
her binoculars.

She did not see a pine siskin.

Mouse giggled.

"That is a pine-*cone.*"

Mole climbed
the tree to get it.

"Spring is about starting *anew*,"
he chuckled. "*I* am starting
a *new* pinecone collection!"
Mole stuffed the
pinecone in his pack.
"Where to now?"
Mouse wondered.
"Birds need water," said Mole.
"Let's go by the pond."
Whoosh! A gust of wind blew
Mole's hat off.
He ran to pick it up.

"A catbird!" Mole pointed.

Mouse looked through her binoculars.

She did not see a catbird.

"Do not be silly, Mole.

Those are cat-*tails!*"

Mouse plucked a daisy.

She stuck it in her bonnet.

*"April showers bring
May flowers!"*
Mouse sang.

Mole took a whistle

from his pocket.

He blew into the end:

Purdy-purdy! it called.

Somewhere a bird sang: *Purdy-purdy!*

Mouse spotted a red bird in the thicket.

"A cardinal!" whispered Mouse.

Mole got out his red crayon.

They crept closer . . .

and closer . . .

Critch-CRUNCH!

Mole stepped on a dried leaf.

The cardinal flew away.

"Rats!" muttered Mole.

He blew into the other end

of the whistle:

Per-chick-o-ree! it called.

Somewhere a bird sang:

Per-chick-o-ree!

Mouse spotted a
small yellow bird
in the grass.
"A goldfinch!"
whispered Mouse.
Mole got out his yellow crayon.
They crept closer . . . and closer . . .
Crick-CRACK!
Mole stepped on a twig.
The goldfinch flew away.
"Double rats!"
muttered Mole.

CRICK-CRACK

He found another
whistle in his pack.
Mole blew into the end:
Queedle-queedle! it called.
Somewhere a bird sang:
Queedle-queedle!
Mouse spotted a large blue bird in
the oak. *"A blue jay!"* whispered Mouse.
Mole got out his blue crayon.
They crept closer . . . and closer . . .
Splish-SPLASH!
Mole stepped in a puddle.
The blue jay flew away.

"Phooey!" grumped Mole. "Birds must
be afraid of *mice!* How will we *ever*
get close enough to draw them?"
Mouse just shook her head.
Mole sat down on the stoop.
Mouse twirled her tail.
"Birds may be afraid
of mice," Mouse began,
"or *maybe* they're
afraid of *moles* . . .
But, birds are not
afraid of birds!"

Mouse told Mole her plan.

"That is a crazy idea!" chuckled Mole.

"Shall we begin in the morning?"
Mouse suggested.

"In the morning,
we begin," agreed Mole.

WHOOSH! A huge gust
of wind blew Mole's
hat into the tree.

MOLEBIRD AND MOUSEBIRD

It was still dark when Mouse knocked
on Mole's door: TAP-TAP-TAP.
"Morning, Mole," said Mouse.
"The early bird gets the worm!"
Mole stretched.
Mole yawned.
"The worms are still
asleep," he mumbled.

Mouse set a box on the table.

"It is time to get busy, Mole!"

She took an old dress from the box.

"First, we cut the cloth

into leaflike shapes."

Mole raised a paw. "What *kind* of

leaf, Mouse? *Oak?*" he said hopefully.

Oak leaves were Mole's favorite.

"Not oak." Mouse smiled.

She held up a willow leaf.

Snip, snip, snip! Mouse cut the
dress into leaflike pieces.
Next, she cut up a red top.

Mole took an old pair of pants.
Snip, snip, snip! Mole cut the
pants into leaflike pieces.
Next, he cut up a green shirt.
"Now what?" said Mole.

Mouse took a sweatshirt from the box.

With a needle and thread,

Mouse sewed a cloth leaf on.

Mole pulled out his sweatshirt.

Mole stared at the scraps of cloth.

"This will take forever!" he gasped.

Mouse twirled her tail.

Mole rubbed his snout.

"I have a *better* idea,"

he announced.

Mole rummaged through the cupboard.

He found a jar of glue.

"Put your sweatshirt on," Mole ordered.

Mouse zipped her sweatshirt up.

"What now?" she said.

Mole spread glue on the front of

Mouse's sweatshirt.

He brushed glue on the back.

Mole handed Mouse the brush.

"Now do me!" he said.

Mouse spread glue on the front of
Mole's sweatshirt.

She brushed glue on the back.

"What now?" said Mouse.

Mole pushed all the cloth leaves off
the table. They made a big mound on
the ground. Mole lay on top of the pile.
Mouse lay down beside him.

Mole and Mouse rolled to the left.

Mouse and Mole rolled to the right.

The scraps of cloth stuck to them like feathers
on a bird! Mole hopped onto the table.
"I am *Molebird!*" he crowed. "See me fly!"
Mole jumped high in the air.
Mole flapped his
arms like mad.

Flippety-flap —
FLUMP!
Mole tumbled to
the ground.

Mouse just shook her head.
"I am *Mousebird,*" she giggled,
"your fine feathered friend."
Molebird gave Mousebird a high-five!

THE NEST

Mouse and Mole circled the oak tree.

Twigs and sticks littered the ground.

"Now that we *look* like birds . . ." said Mole.

"We should *act* like birds," said Mouse.

Mole collected twigs and sticks.

Mouse tied

them in a bundle.

Huff, puff!

They pulled the bundle up into the oak.

Together, Mouse and Mole built a nest.

Whoosh! A gust of wind shook it apart.

Mouse twirled her tail.

Mole rubbed his snout.

He remembered something

about mud and nests.

"I'll be right back!" he said.

Mole scrambled down from

the oak. Mole filled

a bucket with mud.

Together, Mouse and Mole packed
mud between the twigs and sticks.
"Much better!" said Molebird.
"Much, *much* better!" said Mousebird.
They sat down in the nest.
"Ouch!" yelled Mole.
A stick poked Mole's bottom.

"Ouch!" yelped Mouse.
A twig jabbed Mouse in the back.
Mole rubbed his snout.
Mouse twirled her tail.

She remembered something about grass and nests. "I'll be right back!" Mouse scrambled down from the oak. Mouse filled a bucket with grass. Together, Mole and Mouse padded the sides and bottom of the nest.

"Much better!" sighed Mousebird.

"Much, *much* better!" sighed Molebird.

They took out their sketchpads.

Purdy-purdy chirped a red bird.

The cardinal flew down beside them.

Mole nearly toppled out of the nest!

"You were right, Mouse," he whispered.

"Birds are not afraid of other birds!"

Molebird gave Mousebird a low-five.

He opened his box of crayons.

They stood in neat rows by color.

The ends were nice and pointy.

Mole selected a red crayon.

He began to sketch using light strokes.

Mouse dumped her
crayons from the pack.

She picked out the red one.

The end was rounded.

Its paper cover was torn off.

Mouse pressed down hard on the pad.

Snap! The crayon broke in two.

"Whoops!" said Mouse.

Mole was too busy drawing to notice.

After a while, the cardinal flew off.

A black-capped chickadee took its place.

Chick-a-dee-dee-dee! it called.

Mouse liked mimicking bird songs.

"*Chick-a-dee-dee-dee!*" sang Mouse.

Mole was too busy drawing to notice.

All day long birds came and went.

Pretty soon it got too dark to draw.

Mole stretched.

Mole flapped his arms.

"My, how time flies!"

he chuckled.

Mouse and Mole

packed up their things.

They climbed down from the nest.

"Good night, feathered friend,"

said Molebird to Mousebird.

"Good night, feathered friend,"

said Mousebird to Molebird.

SOME ARTIST, SOME POET!

Mole spread his drawings on the floor.

Mouse tacked her pictures to the wall.

Mole looked at Mouse's.

Mouse looked at Mole's.

She stared at the one of a cardinal.

The lines were neatly drawn.

The colors blended smoothly together.

Mole had used mostly red.

He added purple to the shady parts.

There were flecks of orange

in the sunny parts.

Mole's drawing looked so real.
Mouse could imagine
the red bird singing:
Purdy-purdy!

"This is magnificent!" she exclaimed.
Mole blushed a cardinal red.
"You are *some* artist!" Mouse declared.

At the bottom, Mole had printed:

C – a – r – b – i – n – a – l.

The letters were wobbly. Some leaned
to the left; others tilted to the right.

"*Cardinal* is spelled with a *d*,"
Mouse pointed out.

"Whoops!" said Mole. "Sometimes my
letters get flip-flopped," he explained.
"Writing is not my *thing*."

Mole stood by Mouse's picture of
a cardinal. Mouse had printed
C – a – r – d – i – n – a – l
neatly at the top.

A poem was written at the bottom.

Mole read it out loud:

A cardinal is red.
It has a pointy head.
A strong beak it needs
To bust open seeds!

Mole shut his eyes.
He could imagine a seed
in the red bird's beak —
CRACK!

"Did you make that up?" Mole asked.
Mouse shyly nodded yes.
"You are *some* poet!"
declared Mole.
Mouse blushed
a cardinal red.

Mole studied the sketch of the bird.
The lines were all jiggly. "This foot
has seven claws," Mole pointed out.
"Whoops!" said Mouse.

Mouse had colored the red bird orange.
Some purple was scribbled on top.
"My red crayon broke," Mouse explained.
"Drawing is not my *thing*," she added.

Mole looked at Mouse.

Mouse looked at Mole.

"I have another *crazy* idea," she began.

"What if we took *your* pictures
and *my* poems . . ."

"To make one book instead of two?"
Mole hopped to his feet.
He rushed out the
door and down
into his hole.

Mole came back with glue
and more paper.

Mouse fetched scissors,
a needle, and thread.

It was time to get busy!

Step 1: Mouse and Mole cut out
the poems and pictures.

Step 2: Mouse and Mole brushed glue on the backs of both.

Step 3: Mole arranged and pasted everything on new sheets of paper.

Step 4: Mouse stitched the pages together. "Our book is done!" she announced.

"What should we call it?" said Mole.

Mouse twirled her tail. "How about . . .

Mouse and Mole's Bird Book!"

Mole rubbed his snout.

"Perhaps *Mole* **and Mouse's**

Bird Book?" he suggested.

Mouse looked at Mole.

Mole looked at Mouse.

"I know!" he exclaimed.

"We can call it **Feathered Friends**!"

"*Fine* Feathered Friends," Mouse added.

"With *poems* by Mouse," chuckled Mole.

"And *pictures* by Mole," giggled Mouse.

Molebird gave Mousebird

a double high-five!